HUNKY DORY FOUND IT

BY Katie Evans

PICTURES BY Janet Morgan Stoeke

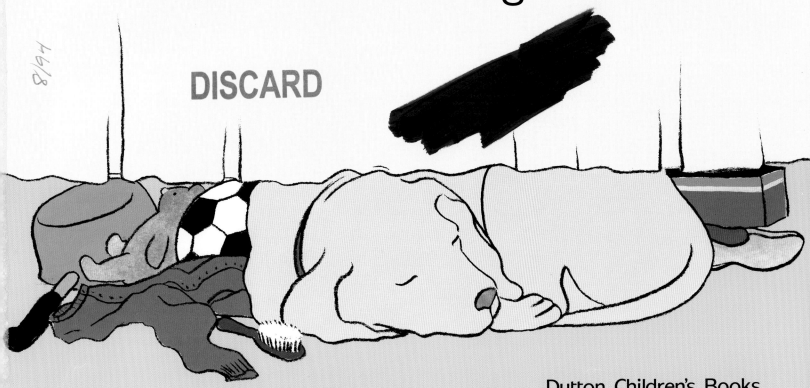

Dutton Children's Books
New York

Text copyright © 1994 by Katie Evans
Illustrations copyright © 1994 by Janet Morgan Stoeke

CIP Data is available.

Published in the United States 1994 by Dutton Children's Books,
a division of Penguin Books USA Inc.
375 Hudson Street, New York, New York 10014

Designed by Riki Levinson

Printed in Hong Kong by South China Printing Co.
First Edition   10 9 8 7 6 5 4 3 2 1
ISBN 0-525-45192-7

For my sisters—Nancy and Julie
K.E.

For Harrison Shaw Brooks
J.M.S.

Sarah Locke
dropped a sock.

Hunky Dory found it.

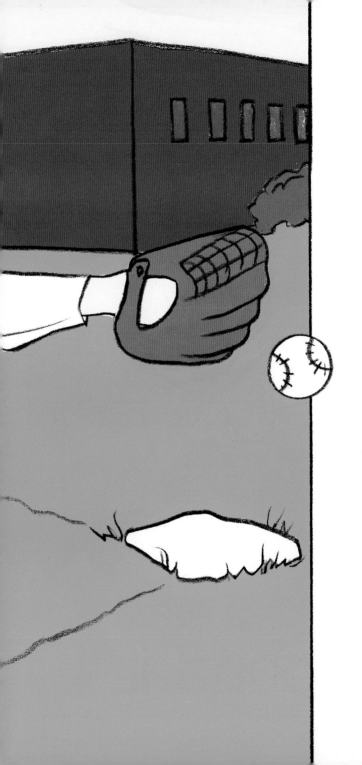

Tommy Hall
hit the ball.

Hunky Dory found it.

Julie Fry
dropped
Daddy's tie.

Hunky Dory found it.

Laurie Cook
put down
her book.

Hunky Dory found it.

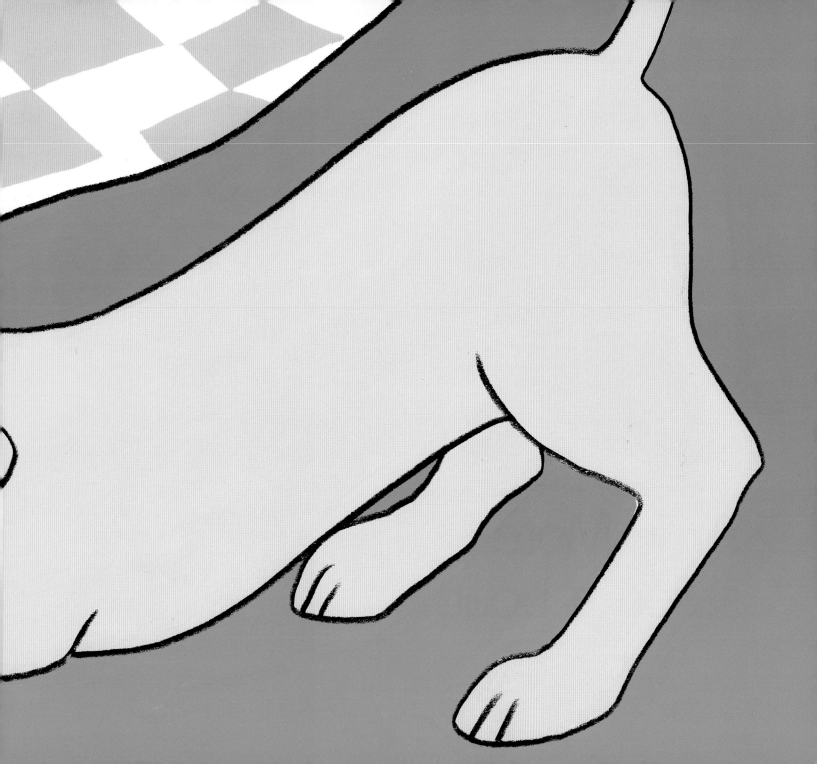

Amy Mote
sailed a boat.

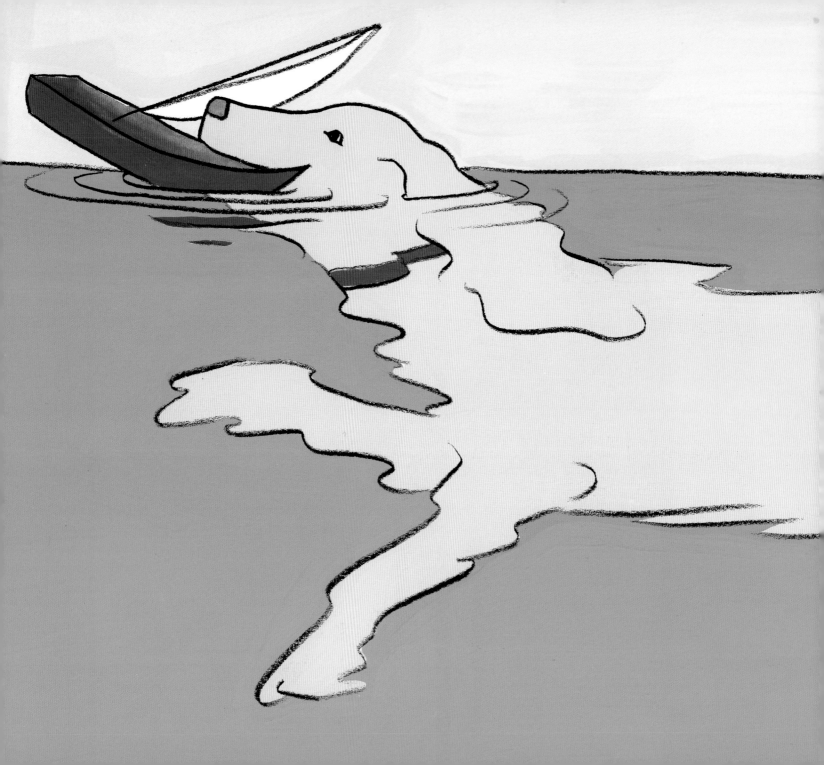

Hunky Dory
found it.

Baby Sue
kicked off
her shoe.

Hunky Dory found it.

Julie shook her head
and frowned
when she saw
what he had found.

She put the treasures
in a sack.

Hunky Dory
took them back.

JP
E   Evans, Katie.
          Hunky Dory found it.